Magical Mozart and his Musical Friends

The Sad Little Violin

Noel and Luz Donegan
Concept by **Aoife O'Reilly**
Illustrated by **Laura Jane Phelan**

VERITAS

Published 2012 by Veritas Publications
7–8 Lower Abbey Street, Dublin 1, Ireland
publications@veritas.ie
www.veritas.ie

ISBN 978-1-84730-393-6

Copyright © Noel and Luz Donegan, 2012
Based on an original concept by Aoife O'Reilly.

10 9 8 7 6 5 4 3 2 1

Designed by Lir Mac Cárthaigh, Veritas
Printed by W&G Baird, Antrim

Veritas books are printed on paper made from the wood
pulp of managed forests. For every tree felled, at least
one tree is planted, thereby renewing natural resources.

The conductor waves his magic baton
and soon all the instruments' troubles are gone.
The upbeat and tuneful fun never ends
with Magical Mozart and his Musical Friends!

Mozart was resting under a tree,
feeling as happy as happy can be.
When all of a sudden and out of nowhere,
the sound of sad sobbing made him rise from his chair.

'Oh, I really am sorry I gave you a start,'
sobbed a sad Violin to a curious Mozart.
'I've been searching so long, looking for you.
Please help me, dear maestro, I don't know what to do.'

'There, there,' said Mozart, 'there's no need to cry.
If you need my help, then of course I will try.
So, little Violin, why are you so sad?
I'm sure when you tell me, things won't seem so bad.'

'You are ever so kind,' sobbed sad Violin,
'but it really is bad. Oh, where to begin?'
And so Violin, with her head hanging low,
began her sad story, as Mozart held her bow.

'I come from a family - they call us the Strings -
where everyone plays and everyone sings.
But when I tried playing for the very first time,
the sounds that I made hurt both their ears and mine!'

'My sister Viola said, "Try it once more,"
as she held open the pages of her musical score.
So I picked up my bow and gave it a try,
but the sound was so awful I started to cry!'

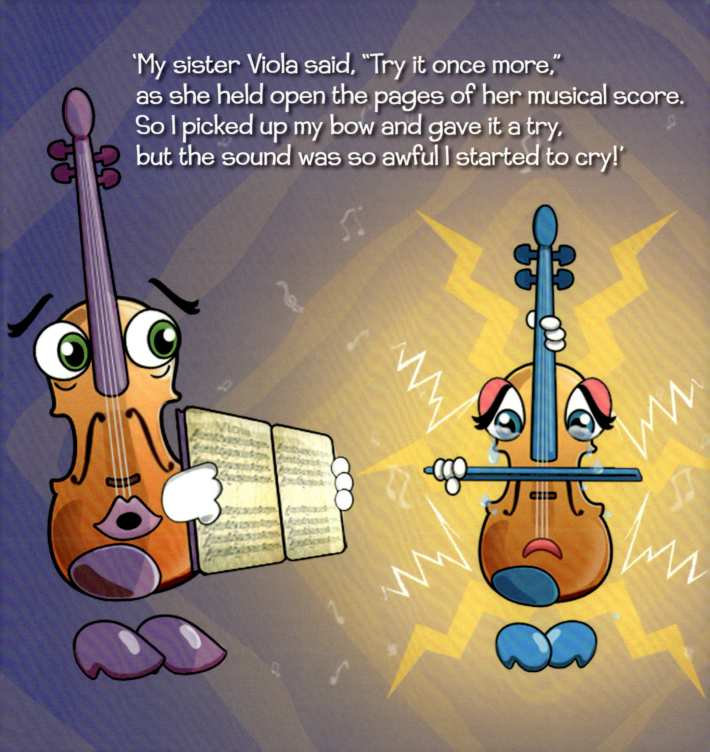

'Then Harp and Cello said, "You must not give in,"
and holding open their scores, urged me to begin.
So I did what they asked and tried hard to play,
but my voice screeched so badly, they both ran away!'

'Double Bass then came over and showed me his score,
saying, "Don't be alarmed, just try it once more."
But he seemed to be sorry when my playing began,
for, with fingers in ears, he turned round and ran!'

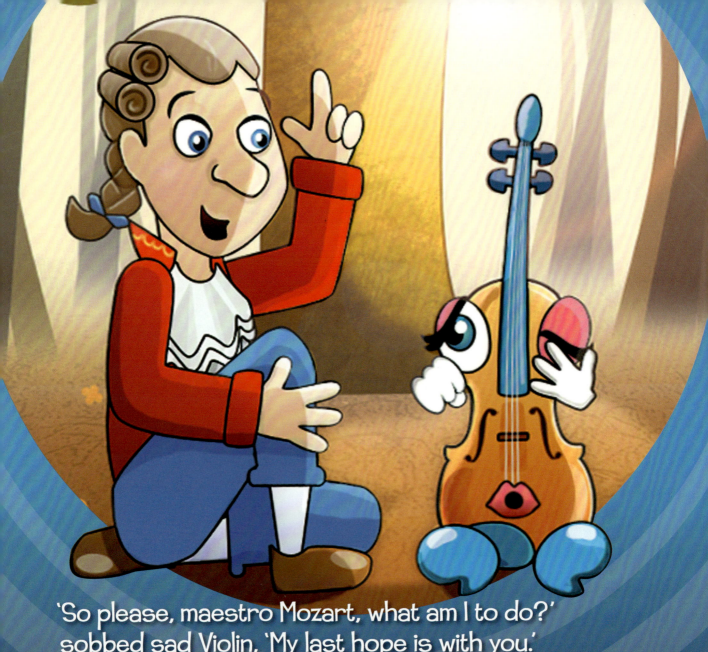

'So please, maestro Mozart, what am I to do?'
sobbed sad Violin, 'My last hope is with you.'
'Well, first wipe those unhappy tears from your eyes,'
Mozart answered back, 'for I've got a surprise.'

'Your problem, my sad little violin friend,
is no problem at all, you will see by day's end!
There are musical things that no instrument knows,
but for now please be quiet, for I need to compose.'

Sad Violin, who had not smiled in a week,
now beamed as she wiped the last tear from her cheek.
Then Mozart, humming, went back to his chair
to compose his great music and pluck notes from the air.

When Mozart had finished he called to Violin,
'I've finished the score, so now let's begin!
Listen to the notes as they dance on your strings.
Each one you can play and each one of them sings.'

'But maestro,' said Violin as she took up her bow,
when you hear how I play you will run off, I know.'
But Mozart just smiled and said, 'Not any more,
you will sing like an angel when you play my score.'

Then, as Mozart listened, Violin played her song
and the notes were so lovely that the birds sang along.
Violin was so happy that she wouldn't stop playing
and her beautiful music set the big oak trees swaying.

'How on earth did you do it?' Violin cried
to a happy Mozart, who was so full of pride.
'How can I play this music you wrote,
when before I could not play even one note?'

'Well, Viola and Cello and Double Bass too,
did their best,' said Mozart, 'to bring music to you.
But each of their scores was composed for their voice,
so when you tried playing them, it didn't sound nice.'

'You cannot be Cello nor can Cello
        be you,
or any other instrument - believe me,
        it's true.
Your sounds are so different and
        that's how it should be,
even though you belong to the same
        String family.'

'Oh, thank you, maestro Mozart,'
  little Violin replied,
'I'm so happy that you heard me
  when I sobbed and I cried.
I've never felt as happy as I
  feel today.
Now I'll run back to my family
  and show them how I play.'

'Not so fast, my little friend, for
    there's more to your surprise,'
Mozart said to Violin, with a twinkle
    in his eyes.
'My orchestra needs a leader, and
    I'd like it to be you.
Now you've found your voice, I ask
    you share it too.'

Mozart waved his baton and the
String family appeared.
And as Double Bass hugged Violin,
Harp and Cello cheered.
Viola was so happy she went into
a spin.
And the orchestra, who had followed,
cried 'Hurray for Violin!'

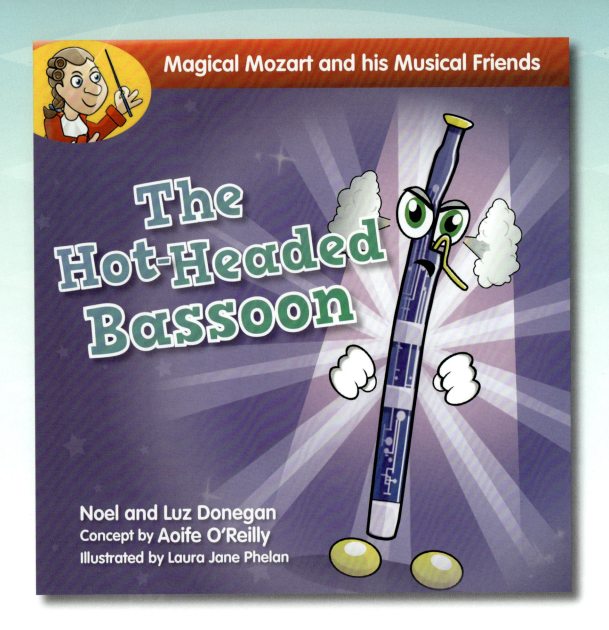

Magical Mozart and his Musical Friends

The Hot-Headed Bassoon

Noel and Luz Donegan
Concept by **Aoife O'Reilly**
Illustrated by Laura Jane Phelan

Also available:

The Hot-Headed Bassoon
(ISBN 978-1-84730-392-9)

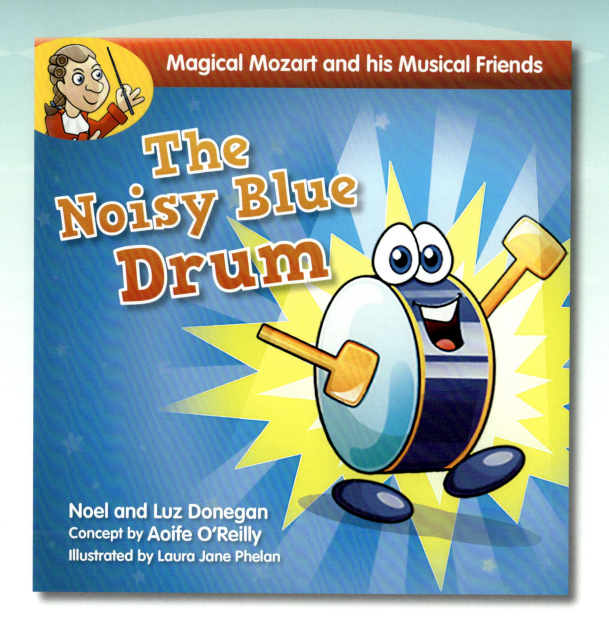

Also available:

The Noisy Blue Drum
(ISBN 978-1-84730-391-2)